Cara's Letters

Story by Kathryn Sutherland
Illustrations by Chantal Stewart

Contents

Chapter 1	A Broken Home	4
Chapter 2	To the City	8
Chapter 3	Grandma's House	10
Chapter 4	A New School	13
Chapter 5	A Visit and a New Job	19
Chapter 6	Back Home	23
Chapter 7	For Sale	25
Chapter 8	A New Beginning	28

A Broken Home

December 26

Dear Megan — my most trusted friend, I hope your winter break is going a lot better than mine. You won't believe what's happened here. I've become a statistic.

Are you ready to hear about THE WORST CHRISTMAS DAY IN HISTORY?

Well, Dad and Mom had a HUGE *fight* right in the middle of dinner — and Mom walked out. We didn't even get to eat dessert! Then Dad hid himself in the bedroom, and James and I were left alone to think about peace and goodwill on Earth.

Mom stormed back in two hours later and there was more shouting — and then Dad left. We haven't seen him since. He has called twice, but can't think what to say to us. I don't think Dad is coming back. I wish all of this had never happened.

So now I'm a child from a broken home — a statistic. I don't know what to do or how to feel. I miss Dad, and Mom is really unhappy. I don't want anyone to know about Mom and Dad breaking up — except you, of course. You're the only person I can talk to about this. Grandma calls twice a day, but she's upset, too. I don't want to dump all my troubles on her.

I wish you were here instead of on vacation at the beach. You always know how to help. Remember when our old tool shed collapsed onto my cottage garden? You came over with boxes of seedlings, and you thought of extending the cottage garden where the shed had been. You were great. I think it'll take more than a few plants to cheer me up this time, but I know if anyone can make me *feel* better, it's you.

Bring me back a big shell that you can hear the sea in, if you can — and some seaweed. I heard on the radio that it's great for compost, and my garden needs a boost. It looks sadly neglected at the moment.

Lots of love,

Cara, the sad statistic

Chapter 2

To the City

December 28

Dear Megan,

Just when I thought things couldn't get any worse... Mom's decided to move back to the city. And WE HAVE TO GO WITH HER!

I can't believe it! I don't want to go and neither does James. I don't want to leave Castleton. I don't want to leave my friends or my school or my dad. I'll miss everyone so much. I'll miss you so much. You've been my best friend since we started school! I don't want to go to some other stupid school where I won't know anybody.

HURRY UP AND COME HOME, MEGAN!

Love,

Cara, the very sad

Chapter 3

Grandma's House

January 4

Dear Megan,

Just a quick note to say thank you, thank you, thank you! The farewell party was awesome. You are the best friend ever.

I got my photos developed as soon as we got here. This one is for you. We're gorgeous, aren't we? Pin it on your wall so you don't forget me. I'll write with details of this place later. Mom's yelling at me to unpack.

Miss you already,

Cara, the gorgeous

January 7

Dear Megan,

Thanks for the photos. I've stuck them all over my door. You look crazy in half of them, but that makes sense... you are crazy!

Grandma's house is pretty boring. It used to be fun coming here for holidays, but living here feels different. I've got Aunt Tina's old room. It's very girly — floral curtains, lots of pink, and frilly things everywhere. Not my style at all. Mom won't let me cover the walls with magazine cut-outs like I did in my old room.

James is in Grandpa's old office — very brown and boring, but that should suit him well. Ha ha!

Actually there's not much to laugh about here. Mom still cries a lot. James has gotten really quiet — something to be thankful for, I guess. Grandma's been good. She gives us all lots of hugs. James pretends he hates it, but I can see him squeezing her back.

Dad hasn't called ONCE yet. Grandma thinks he's scared of what she'll say to him. But I miss him so much and wish he'd call.

I miss you, too.

Love,

Cara of the frilly pink room (YUCK)

Chapter 4

A New School

January 9

Dear Megan,

Well, it had to happen. We started at our new school today. It's enormous, with three times as many kids as at Castleton. How will I ever get to know anyone?

I was given a buddy named Sarah. She's showing me around the school and looking after me this week. I'm not sure she's enjoying it though. I feel like a nobody in this huge place.

James got in a fight at lunch time. I don't think it was his fault. Some bully just decided to pick on him because he's new. Mom had to come to see the principal. You can imagine how she felt about that! Still, it meant we got a ride home instead of having to walk.

How are things at Castleton? Are you going to run for student council president? You should. There won't be much competition now that I'm not there. (JOKE!) I wouldn't have a hope here. No one knows me from a bar of soap.

Write soon.

Love,

Cara, the invisible

P.S. Dad called finally. We had a good talk.

January 25

Dear Megan,

What should I call you now? ... Oh, great one? Megan the magnificent? President Meg? WELL DONE! I knew you'd do it!

School here is okay, I guess. A few kids talk to me now and then. Our teacher is pretty cool. His name is Mr. Pentel. Some VERY FUNNY kids call him Mr. Pencil. Ha ha.

Such sophisticated humor here — much classier than in country Castleton, I DON'T THINK! I've decided I'm no less cool than these city kids. I don't feel different, and I don't look different.

Mom has invited Sarah over "to play" tomorrow afternoon. Can you believe she said that? — "to play!" How old does she think I am? I was so embarrassed. Anyway, Sarah said yes, so now I guess I'll have to think of something to play!

James has made one friend. Guess who it is? The guy who bashed him the first day! Boys are so crazy.

Got to go so I can get this letter in tonight's mail. I've got lots of homework to do for Mr. Pencil (whoops!).

See you, President,

Love,

Cara, the player

Chapter 5

A Visit and a New Job

February 26

Dear President Meg,

Sorry I haven't written for a while. Dad came down to the city for three whole weeks! It was FANTASTIC! He didn't stay with us, but he took James and me out a lot. We went to the movies and to restaurants on the weekend and even after school a couple of times. He also took us away fishing one weekend, which was great.

We tried to get Dad and Mom to go out together, but Mom wouldn't even see him. James and I hope they will get back together eventually, but Mom says no. They did manage to have a telephone conversation or two without yelling at each other, though, which is something.

Well, Meg, old pal, I hope YOUR family's all doing well.

Love,

Cara, the curious

March 12

Dear Megan,

Thanks for another fabulous letter. I love catching up on news of Castleton and how you boss the school around.

Mom seems a bit better lately. She still looks sad most of the time, but she yells at us a lot less, WHICH IS GOOD! She got a job last week! It's in the middle of the city, so she takes the train in. She looks so cool dressed in a business suit and high heels. Dad would be really proud of her if he saw her.

I have to go over to Sarah's. We're doing a project together. I have to admit it — Sarah and I are becoming pretty good friends. But don't worry, President Megan. You are my BEST friend and always will be. Can't wait to see you when we visit during spring break!

Love,

Cara, the project queen

Chapter 6

Back Home

April 10

Dear Megan,

It was SOOOOOO good to see you last weekend.
I loved being home in Castleton — even though
it wasn't in our old home.

When we got back, Mom was full of
questions about Dad: how he seemed, what his
new place was like, whether he was happy, etc.
She stared a long time at the photo you took of
him, James, and me on his porch.

The old gang seems about the same. I probably raved too much about life in the city and bored everyone stupid. Sorry, I didn't mean to. You know I LOVE Castleton. I still have all your photos pinned up on my door.

Ask your parents if you can come and stay this summer. Then I can show you all the places I raved about.

Hope school's okay.

See you.

Love,

Cara, the raver

Chapter 7

For Sale

June 24

Dear Megan,

They're selling our house! Can you believe it?

How dare they! The people who have been renting our house in Castleton this year want to buy it, and Mom and Dad have agreed to sell!

How can they do that to me? How can they sell my childhood home? The house where James and I were babies. The garden we worked so hard on, that became so beautiful. It was bad enough knowing strangers were sleeping in my bedroom and eating in our kitchen, but now they'll be living there forever. I will never be able to take my own children there for holidays and tell them about things I did as a kid in that house. Unfair!

The worst thing is, it means that Mom and Dad will not be getting back together. Ever!

Can you ask your parents if THEY'LL buy the house? Then you could live there, and I could come to visit and sleep in my old bedroom! I know YOU'D take care of the garden.

Love,

Cara, the homeless

Chapter 8

A New Beginning

August 12

Dear Megan,

Sorry it's been so long since I wrote. So much has happened and I've been really busy.

I told you on the phone we were moving. Well, here we are! We're just around the corner from Grandma's place: twelve houses to be exact. We can stay at the same school, which is good.

I didn't mind living at Grandma's — apart from the GROSS pink bedroom — but we couldn't stay there forever. Grandma took care of us totally, but I think she was happy to see us go, especially since we're just around the corner.

Our new house isn't nearly as big as the one we had in Castleton. Houses are much more expensive here — plus Mom had to share the money from the house sale with Dad.

This little house is quite old and was a bit of a dump when we first moved in, but we've painted it and it looks much better already.

This weekend we'll start on the garden. There's a beautiful big maple tree in the yard, but not much else, so we've got lots of digging and planting to do. Sarah's mom has given us lots of plants. She works at the local nursery. Sarah and I are going to the beach this afternoon to collect some seaweed for the compost.

Oh, I didn't tell you about my room. It's green — like an indoor garden — apart from all my magazine cut-outs which, I'm pleased to say, are back! And yes, I still have plenty of photos of the Castleton gang on my door.

Write soon.

Love,

Cara, the interior decorator

P.S. I think we're going to be okay in this house. It has a good 'feel' to it.

November 26

Hi Megan,

I'm so happy you're coming to visit over winter break — I can't wait to introduce you to Sarah. I know you'll like her and I've told her everything about you. I've got a bunch of stuff to show you. This Christmas will surely be a thousand times better than last year's!

Thanks for being a wonderful friend, President Meg. I don't know how I would have gotten through the events of the past year without your letters and phone calls. You're the best — THE VERY BEST.

Forever your friend.

Love,

Cara, the cool, calm, and congenial (that's one of this week's vocabulary words).